T0365366

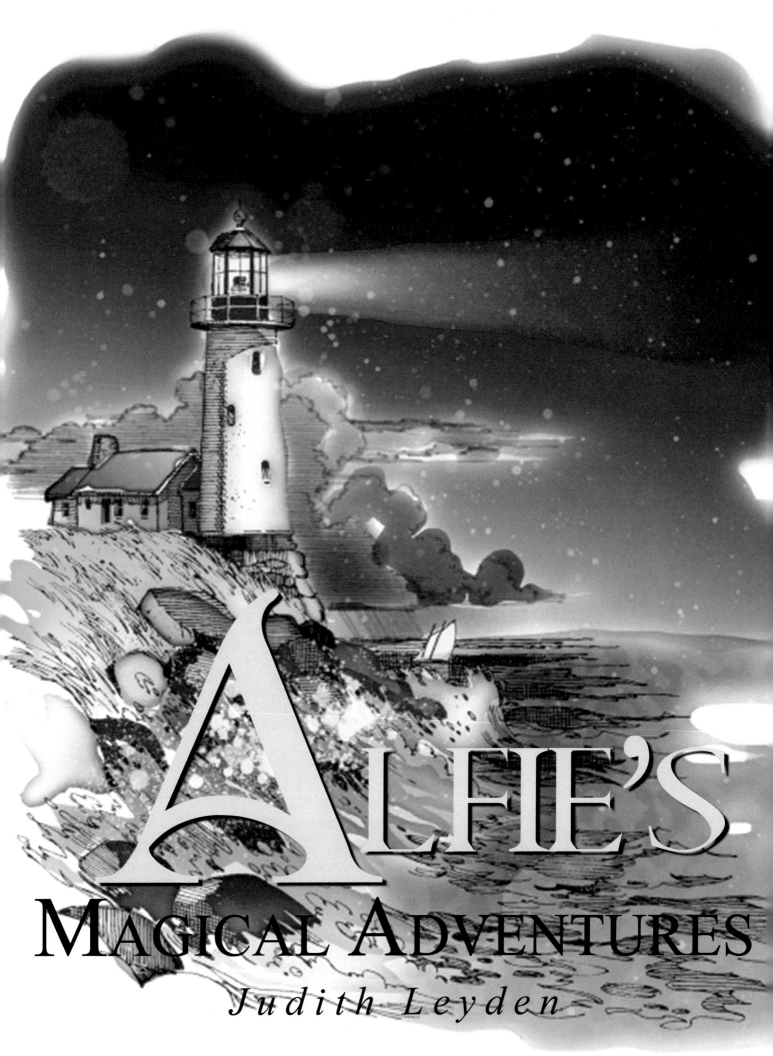

AuthorHouse™ UK Ltd.
1663 Liberty Drive
Bloomington, IN 47403 USA
www.authorhouse.co.uk
Phone: 0800.197.4150

Published by AuthorHouse 01/30/2014

ISBN: 978-1-4918-9267-1 (sc)
ISBN: 978-1-4918-9268-8 (e)

Library of Congress Control Number 2014902096

authorHOUSE®

CHAPTER 1

Leaving London

It was a warm Sunday morning when Alfie and his mother were saying goodbye to their friends and neighbours, they were catching a train from London to Scotland then a boat to the old lighthouse where his uncle Thomas lived. Alfie's mother was a nurse and had decided to transfer to a hospital in Scotland away from London, there was talk on the radio that the Germans were going to drop bombs on London, as Alfie's father was away fighting in the war his mother thought it was best for Alfie to stay with his uncle until the war was over away from London and the bombs, sadly Alfie didn't agree with his mother, being a inquisitive nine year old boy he wanted to stay with his friends, he couldn't think of anything more exciting then bombs falling on London. His mother had promised Alfie a comic and sweets for the journey if he was good so he waved goodbye to his friends, picked up his small brown suitcase to carry and quietly walked to the train station with his mother beside him, she looked at him smiled and said "cheer up Alfie dear just think of it as a big adventure", "I will try mother" he replied.

St Pancreas train station was enormous to a small child of nine, Alfie had never been inside the station or on a train before, maybe mother was right he thought to himself this is exciting. He had never seen so many people in one place there were men in uniform like his father and nurses like his mother waiting to board the huge trains on the platforms, large boxes and parcels being loaded onto the trains, steam covering the ceiling above their heads as the trains pulled out of the station. Alfie was so amazed with it all he didn't hear his mother calling him, "Alfie come here and choose what sweets and comic you would like for the journey" as he turned around he saw a small shop next to the tea shop where his mother was waiting for him, "isn't it wonderful mother" he said as he chose lemon sherbet sweets and a dandy comic "yes dear it is" she replied "come along now we have to board our train".

As the train journey began Alfie looked out of the window watching the train depart from the station slowing leaving London he felt a little sad again but soon was enjoying seeing all the different places as they past by, he had never seen so many cows and fields in one day but the journey was long and alfie soon got bored with looking out of the window so mother shared their sandwiches she had made and gave alfie his sweets and comic to read while he ate, after a few hours alfie grew tired and fell asleep with his head on his mothers lap.

CHAPTER 2

Uncle Thomas Lighthouse

Alfie woke as the train stopped, they had arrived in Scotland, he felt much better after his sleep and excited again for he remembered to reach Uncle's lighthouse they have to get on a boat and Alfie had never been on a boat, well not a proper boat just a rowing boat on the pond at the park where his father had taken him for a treat before he left to fight in the war. Alfie and his mother collected their suitcases, walked out of the train station straight to the port. When they had reached the port his uncle was waiting for them with a small boat of his own, which he used often for his work in the war. Alfie's mother gave her brother a hug and introduced him to Alfie " this is your uncle Thomas Alfie dear", uncle Thomas smiled at Alfie and shook his hand " it's wonderful to see you again laddie, you were a wee baby the last time I saw you and now nearly a grown man". Alfie looked up to see his uncle smiling down at him, he had scruffy brown hair like Alfie's under his cap, " come aboard my wee boat we need to get home before it's dark". Alfie and his mother climbed aboard the boat, his uncle put the suitcases away then he put a padded sleeveless jacket on Alfie while his mother put one on herself, " a lifebuoy is what that's called laddie", uncle explained " so if you fall overboard you wont drown", Alfie's face went pale, " don't worry dear" his mother said " you wont fall overboard the jacket is for your safety only". Alfie sat down on the seat and held tight to the rope attached to the boat. Uncle Thomas's small boat went fast across the water, after a while Alfie relaxed and started to enjoy himself, they finally arrived at uncle Thomas's lighthouse.

The lighthouse was large and round all the way to the light at the top, with a small cottage attached to the side, there was a small beach with rocks and a cave on one side " you can play as much as you like down here laddie" said his uncle, " but don't go into the cave unless the tide is out or you will be stranded for days", "ok uncle Thomas", replied Alfie who couldn't wait to explore the small island. Inside the lighthouse were stairs leading to the bedrooms, and the large light at the very top, " never go up to the top Alfie", said his mother, " it is important, your uncle's war work is to maintain the light in working order to direct our ships on the sea", " yes mother ", Alfie replied "I promise". Downstairs the room was large with a kitchen, table and chairs, a settee in front of the small open fire and a room at the back where uncle Thomas slept. Alfie was told never to go into, which he promised, poor Alfie was beginning to think there was nowhere he could play and sadly no other boy to play with. "I have a wireless you can listen to all your favourite programmes, and lots of games and puzzles we can do together", said his uncle trying to cheer him up and your mother will be back to stay soon". Alfie's mother was a nurse and she was returning to the mainland early tomorrow morning to begin her new post at the hospital, "I'll be home as often as I can Alfie dear', said his mother', "I promise". Alfie and his mother spent the evening playing together, but it was soon bedtime, he said goodnight to them both and slept soundly in his new bed.

CHAPTER 3

The Penny Whistle

Alfie woke up early the next morning to say goodbye to his mother, his uncle was taking her in his boat back across to the mainland and picking up supplies from the stores, " be very good for your uncle Thomas Alfie dear", said his mother as she was going, "I will see you soon". Alfie gave his mother a big hug and waved goodbye until he could no longer see the boat, he then went back inside the lighthouse to finish his breakfast. After washing up his plate and mug and making his bed Alfie decided to explore the small island remembering what his uncle had told him, not to go inside the cave.

The island was mainly grass and lots of rocks to climb which is what Alfie did being a typical nine year old boy, very slowly Alfie climbed and climbed the rocks as high as he could, he tried climbing as high as the light at the top of the lighthouse, the view across the ocean went on for miles and miles to Alfie that was a very long way, the sun was shinning brightly as he imagined looking for German ships, suddenly he saw something near the rocks along the beach, he climbed down slowly making sure not to slip and ran down to the beach to get a closer look, he searched in between the small rocks and stones along the water front, he then took off his shoes and socks to wade in and out of the water hoping to find something, to his surprise there was something stuck between the rocks and it wasn't seaweed.

Alfie bent down getting his knees slightly wet to pick up the floating object, he couldn't quite make out what it was, he thought it was a small piece of wood, then realised it was shiny underneath the muddy sand. At that moment he saw his uncle had returned from the mainland, " Alfie boy come and help me with these supplies", his uncle shouted to him, quickly putting his shoes and socks back on Alfie placed the object into his pocket to go and help his uncle.

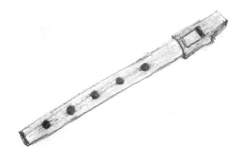

Once inside the lighthouse Alfie showed his uncle what he had found, "I'm not sure what it is laddie", said his uncle, "wash the mud of carefully so we can have a better look". Alfie proceeded to do as his uncle suggested and carefully washed the object, I'm right he thought to himself it is shiny, but he still did not know what it was. "Lets have a closer look then", said his uncle as Alfie placed the object onto the table, "why it's an old penny whistle", exclaimed his uncle, "it's made of tin that's why it's shiny, here use this polish and rag, you will soon have it looking like new". Feeling very pleased with his find Alfie carefully polished the whistle, "look uncle Thomas", he said, 'just like new, "that's grand Alfie", replied uncle Thomas, "now off you go outside to learn to play the whistle while I do some important work", "ok I will'.

CHAPTER 4

The Magic

Once outside Alfie tried blowing into the whistle, but no sound came, he blew harder and harder but still no sound, he walked down to the beach, sat down on the sand and tried again, still no sound came from the whistle, feeling very disappointed Alfie put the whistle back into his pocket, he thought it must be broken, suddenly he heard a dog barking, Alfie looked up and couldn't believe his eyes standing there right in front of him was a small brown dog wagging it's tail, Alfie called to the dog, "here boy", the dog came and jumped onto Alfie's lap, licking him all over his face, "good boy", said Alfie stroking his back, where did you come from he stood and called out, "hello is anybody there, I have your dog", but there was no answer, suddenly the dog grabbed Alfie's trouser leg and pulled him to follow him, "ok boy show me", the dog ran ahead towards the cave, "no boy not in there" ,shouted Alfie, but the dog didn't come back no matter how many times Alfie called him. Against his uncle's warning Alfie decided to go inside the cave just to look for the dog, as he entered he heard music and like magic a Funfair appeared, just like the one he went to with his parents in London before the war, there was a Helter Skelter ride, a swing boat ride, a Carousel ride and a big wheel, he could smell candy floss and hot dogs too.

Alfie thought he was dreaming until the dog licked his hand, "there you are boy", he said, a man called over to him, "come on son it's free to ride all day, what would you like to go on first", "oh the Helter Skelter ride please", said Alfie, he picked up the mat, ran up the stairs, placed the mat down, sat on it and pushed himself down the Helter Skelter ride. Alfie went round and round until he reached the bottom with a bump, "that was terrific mister", he said, "can I go again", in fact Alfie went on the ride several times but he became dizzy so decided to go on the swing boats, the dog jumped inside the ride with Alfie, "you would like a ride too boy", he said, "ok lets go". He pulled on the rope hard as he could which made the ride swing to and fro, the more Alfie pulled the more the ride swung higher and higher until the dog began to bark, "ok boy shall we stop now", said Alfie.

His stomach started to rumble with the lovely smell of hotdogs and candy floss," I'm hungry dog are you, lets try a hotdog, they both jumped down off the swing to the hotdog stand," two hotdogs please", Alfie said and gave one to dog "here you are boy", they sat on the ground and ate, "that was the best tasting hotdog ever," Alfie said looking at dog "come on boy lets go on the big wheel". Alfie raced over to the big wheel, but dog wasn't allowed to go on the ride so waited for Alfie on the ground. Alfie loved the big wheel it made him feel like he was flying high in the sky, but he soon got bored so decided to go on the Carousel ride and then do it all over again and again, he was having so much fun that he didn't hear dog barking at first, "what's wrong boy", he said bending down to stroke him, just then his penny whistle fell out of his pocket, " oh I forgot I had it in my pocket, it doesn't work dog listen", as Alfie blew the whistle just like magic the Funfair disappeared in front of his eyes, he looked down at his penny whistle and realised it didn't play music because it was a magic whistle and when he looked up again dog had gone too.

Alfie ran all the home to his uncle in the lighthouse, who had finished his work and was making supper for them both, "wash your hands ready for supper Alfie then tell me what you have been doing," did you manage to get the penny whistle to work ' asked uncle' Alfie told his uncle the penny whistle was magic and how a little brown dog appeared to show him how to find the magical Funfair where he played all day. "What great imagination you have laddie" said his uncle, come on lets clear away the plates and listen to the wireless", "ok uncle" Alfie replied. When the programme on the wireless had finished Alfie went up to bed "good night uncle" he said "good night laddie" replied uncle 'sleep well', and Alfie did dreaming of the wonderful magical day he had and what other wonderful adventures he will have thanks to his magical penny whistle.

CHAPTER 5
The Next Day

The very next day Alfie was woken by his uncle Thomas 'morning laddie," he said "how about you helping your uncle today, I need to give my motor boat a new coat of paint. "Sure thing uncle" replied Alfie, "I'll be up in a jiffy".

Alfie yawned and stretched, then got out of bed, as he was getting dressed he looked down at the penny whistle on the table, I wonder he thought to himself did I really play at the magical Funfair yesterday or have I just had a lovely dream. Alfie didn't have time to find out, straight after breakfast he went down to the beach to help his uncle. "Ah there you are Alfie", said uncle "lets get started, put this old shirt of mine on to protect your clothes, I don't want a telling off from your mother next time she visits," he said laughing, Alfie did as he was asked and put on his uncle's old shirt, he had to roll up the sleeves as the shirt was a lot bigger then he was. Together they climbed aboard the boat and started to paint. Alfie stayed on the boat painting around the inside, while his uncle painted the outside of the boat.

When the job was done which took all morning Alfie and his uncle sat down to have lunch together," that was a grand job you did Alfie", said his uncle "thank you very much for your help the painting was finished a lot quicker with two, I'm so glad you came to stay with me," he smiled, "I'll wash these few things up and then I need to do some work in the back room," "ok uncle" said Alfie who didn't mind being on his own as he did spent most of his time with his uncle, he enjoyed listening to the wireless and playing games with him in the evening but during the day his uncle was busy with his work for the war, luckily for Alfie he had his penny whistle and decided to try again to play a tune on it, hoping his adventure yesterday wasn't just a dream.
Alfie walked down to the beach where the cave was, he sat down on the sand and blew into the whistle, again no sound came but the little brown dog appeared "dog", Alfie said stroking it's head "how wonderful to see you again boy, where are we going today?' Just like before dog ran into the cave, where Alfie followed.

Once inside the cave Alfie saw a huge castle with a moat full of water all around it, Alfie had never seen a real castle before, only in a picture book at school. The castle was made of stone with five huge towers with flags flying at the top of long poles and a door over the bridge which was wooden, just then the drawbridge came down and a knight on horseback came galloping towards him, "you boy cometh here," bellowed the knight "I need a page to help me with my armour, I am to joust in the tournament against the fierce black knight, bring your companion with you," he said looking down at dog, then he galloped back inside the castle. "Well dog," said Alfie,"I'm not sure what a page is but I'm game if you are." So Alfie and dog followed the knight over the drawbridge into the castle, to Alfie's amazement they were still outside, there was no roof to the castle but stairs leading to four towers. There were tents of all colours everywhere, a long wooden fence in the middle of the grass and wooden benches along the sides for people to sit on, there were stalls with food, flags, swords, and horses and lots of people all dressed in funny clothes. "Cometh boy", said the knight "taketh my horse and tie him to the pole, I am the red knight, sir Richard is my name." "My name is Alfie sir and this is dog", he replied. "Will you be my page?" Asked the red knight, "yes sir", said Alfie "I will".

"This is my tent where I keep my armour and lance", said Sir Richard, "you need to look after them they are my colours of red," "please sir", said Alfie "what is a lance?" "Have you never paged for a knight before boy," he asked. "No sir", alfie sheepishly replied. "Never mind I will teach you". Suddenly from nowhere another knight appeared, he was quite scary, he stopped in front of Alfie and looked down at dog. "I wish to have your companion", he said to Alfie, ", he belongs beside me". "No I am sorry but dog belongs to me", replied Alfie. "Be off with you black knight", said sir Richard, "you are not welcome here, leave my page be". "I will fight you and win, then claim dog to be mine" the knight shouted angrily as he rode away.

"Do not worry yourself page, I will win the match, so you can keep your companion", said Sir Richard, "cometh I need help with my armour". Alfie helped Sir Richard with his armour, it was very heavy, it took a lot of lifting to place on the knight. "Good my boy, now help me on my horse". Struggling Alfie managed to help the red knight onto his horse, Alfie was very pleased with himself, "now pass me my lance." said Sir Richard pointing to a long pole, so Alfie lifted it to him, which he placed into a strap attached to his armour. "Cometh and stand by my side to watch the jousting page", said sir Richard, so Alfie walked by his side to the arena.

The red knight galloped into the arena where the black knight was waiting for him, they placed their horses at opposite ends of each other, holding the heavy lances up high, the knights charged, knocking each other so they would fall off their horses, the one who stays on their horse wins the contest.

Alfie thought the jousting very exciting as he watched the horse's race towards each other while the knights tried plunging each other with their lances, especially when after the fourth attempt the red knight knocked the black knight off his horse. The black knight fell heavily to the ground with a large thump, unable to get up again as the armour was too heavy to lift by himself, making the red knight the winner. Alfie cheered and cheered for the red knight he was so pleased he had won. "Well done sir", he said while helping him off his horse and out of his armour, "thank you page", Sir Richard replied "here is a token of my gratitude for your help today", he took a ring off his small finger and gave it to alfie, it had a red flag on it, "oh thank you Sir Richard", said alfie "you are very kind. "Nonsense my boy you earned it," he replied, "now cometh and eat you must be of hunger".

Alfie and sir Richard sat down and ate together laughing out loud as the black knight had to be carried slowly to his tent, "that was fantastic sir," said Alfie, "you are very brave to fight the black knight". "It is what I do", said Sir Richard "I would not be the red knight if I did not challenge the black knight".

Dog started to bark at Alfie to let him know it was time to go, thanking sir Richard again Alfie said goodbye and walked back over the drawbridge, he took out his penny whistle and blew, once again everything slowly disappeared leaving Alfie back in the cave, he bent down to stroke dog one more time, "see you again soon boy", he said then dog was gone.

Alfie smiled as he placed his magical penny whistle back inside his pocket, not forgetting the ring the red knight had given to him, something to remind him of the wonderful day he had being a page for the amazing red knight.

Alfie returned to the lighthouse in time to make supper for him and uncle Thomas who was still working in the back room. He went upstairs to his bedroom and placed the ring inside his secret box his father had made for him for his birthday, it was made of wood and only Alfie knew you had to tap the lid twice to open it. I will keep this ring secret forever he said, feeling very happy now he knew for sure his penny whistle was magical.

He went back downstairs to make supper "it will be ready in five minutes", Alfie shouted to his uncle though the door, "right laddie" said uncle. They both sat down at the table to eat. Alfie just being nine years old could only make boiled egg and soldiers, "this is wonderful Alfie", said uncle I haven't had boiled egg and soldiers for quite a while, but yours are the best I've ever tasted".

After supper they both listened to the wireless then played games, as Alfie got up to go to bed his uncle turned to him and said "you have to start school soon on the mainland laddie, your mother will be home to take you on your first day, you will have to stay with her all week while you are at school, but you will be back here every weekend". "Ok uncle;" replied Alfie, "it will be lovely to spend some time with mother but I will miss you". But most of all he thought to himself I will miss my adventures. "We still have a few weeks together laddie," said his uncle, "but you will not be able to see your mother until then sorry". "I don't mind honestly uncle," said Alfie he then hugged him and went to bed.

CHAPTER 6
Going To The Mainland

Today after breakfast Alfie and his uncle Thomas were going to the mainland to buy a few supplies, new shoes and a new coat for when he started school, it was a lot colder in Scotland then it was in London, Alfie's old coat would not be warm enough when the snow came, which alfie was looking forward to very much. "Are you ready laddie", his uncle shouted up the stairs, "I'm coming uncle", he replied.

Alfie was looking forward to going to the mainland today, as he had not been off the island for weeks now, he had been having fun with his uncle, to busy even for a magical adventure. They went swimming in the sea and rock climbing together while the weather was hot, "it will soon be snowing laddie, so lets make the most of the lovely sunshine", his uncle suggested, and that's what they did, they swam everyday and yesterday uncle Thomas took Alfie fishing in his boat, they spent the whole day on the boat taking sandwiches with them. Alfie had never fished in the sea before, only by the river with his father, he didn't catch a fish then but yesterday was different, with the help of his uncle Alfie to his surprise caught a fish, which his uncle cooked for supper that evening. It was the tastiest fish alfie had ever eaten, especially as his uncle made some chips, which is Alfie's favourite food to eat with the fish.

Alfie and uncle Thomas had lots of fun together, Alfie loved his uncle very much and thought moving to the lighthouse was the best thing he and his mother had done. Alfie missed his mother but was to see her soon as she was coming home to spend the weekend with him and his uncle, and then Alfie was to start school.

Alfie climbed aboard the boat with his uncle and they set off for the mainland, Alfie enjoyed going on his uncle's boat very much, he found it exciting every time. They quickly reached the mainland at the port Alfie and his mother had arrived, many weeks ago. Alfie never saw any shops when they had first arrived as it was late and they needed to reach his uncle's lighthouse before dark, so he was looking forward to going inside all of them today. "Right laddie", said his uncle "let's start with a good warm coat for you". "Ok", replied Alfie.

They came to a shop full of coats for sale, "there's so many to choose from", Alfie said to his uncle in dismay. He really didn't want to spend too much time looking for things he needed for school, he was hoping to go into the toyshop and the sweet shop more. "Don't worry laddie", said uncle Thomas, "I know the right coat for you", he took a thick duffle coat of the hanger and passed it to Alfie "here laddie try this one on". Alfie did as he was told and put the coat on. He went to the mirror for a closer look, the coat was really smart, it had long thick buttons Alfie had never seen before, they looked like whales teeth Alfie had seen in a book his uncle had given to him to read. "I like this uncle", he said, "that's grand Alfie", replied uncle Thomas, "we're take this one", he said to the man behind the counter. Uncle Thomas paid the man and they left to go into the next shop which was a shoe shop much to Alfie's disappointment as he could clearly see the toyshop across the road. Once inside the shop his uncle asked for a pair of strong sturdy boots for Alfie in his size, Alfie quickly tried them on, "mother said new shoes, not boots uncle", said Alfie, "no laddie ", replied his uncle "you need sturdy boots especially when the snow comes". "Oh ok", said Alfie happily he was looking forward to playing in the snow.

After they had left the shoe shop his uncle decided to buy the supplies they needed for the lighthouse, Alfie felt slightly fed up he was looking forward to the shops but not so many boring ones? Uncle Thomas notice Alfie's sad face, "ah cheer up laddie" he said "how about when we have finished ordering all the supplies we go into the sweet shop and get some sweets and perhaps some icecream for after supper this evening". Alfie looked up to his uncle and smiled "yes please uncle", he said "and could we also have a look in the toy shop pleaseeee', "ok laddie lets do that as soon as we have finished all our shopping". To Alfie it took forever to finish the shopping but finally he and uncle were inside the toyshop. There were toys everywhere cars, aeroplanes, boats, dolls (not that Alfie was interested in them), toy soldiers, puzzles and much more. "I think this is the best shop of all", he said to his uncle, I think you are right laddie, I've never seen so many great toys in one place," uncle replied smiling, "you take your time looking around Alfie". Alfie spent ages looking and sometimes playing if it was allowed with the toys, he had so much fun choosing which ones he liked best, he found a toy racing car which reminded Alfie of when he and his father played together, it made Alfie feel a little sad thinking of his father as he had not seen him in a long time because of the war. His uncle saw that Alfie looked sad and said, "how about we go next door to the café and have a milkshake and a cup of tea, hoping to cheer him up, "yes please uncle", said Alfie, "thank you'.

Once they were sitting down his uncle ordered the drinks he turned to Alfie and said "what's up laddie are you missing your mother, because if you are I am sure we could pop over to the hospital for five minutes to see her'. "I'm sorry uncle Thomas", said Alfie "I was thinking of father, I do miss him so, of cause you do Alfie it's only natural to miss both your parents, you have been absolutely marvellous staying with me away from your parents and the life you know, but I love being with you uncle Thomas," Alfie quickly replied "I know that laddie", said his uncle 'and I like having you, I am sure you will see your father soon and we know he is always thinking of you". Alfie smiled at his uncle and finished his drink, "lets buy a steak and kidney pie for supper tonight on the way back to the boat for a treat", said uncle "we better get a move on the supplies will be delivered to the boat soon".

As Alfie walked back to the boat beside his uncle he thought how lucky he was. After the supplies were boarded they returned to the lighthouse, and after helping his uncle to unpack the shopping, Alfie hung his new coat and placed his new boots inside his wardrobe. He set the table for supper, which was scrumptious steak and kidney pie and icecream afterwards, yummy he thought to himself feeling completely full. Alfie and his uncle sat down quietly and listened to the wireless until bedtime.

Lying in bed Alfie thought what fun he has playing with his uncle, just like the magical adventures. Alfie fell asleep thinking of the new friends he will make when he starts his new school, but most of all he was looking forward to seeing his mother again.

CHAPTER 7

Animal Safari

It was early Saturday morning and Alfie was already up and dressed, his mother was coming to stay it had been many weeks since Alfie had seen his mother so he was very excited. Alfie tidied his room, had breakfast, washed his mug and plate up, then sat down in the chair waiting and watching the big grandfather clock, but the time was going so slowly, too slow until his uncle would return from the mainland with his mother, I'll go for a walk on the beach and wait there for uncle Thomas's boat.

Alfie soon got bored looking out to sea waiting for the boat to return, I know he thought to himself I will see if dog can come and play for a while. He took his penny whistle out of his pocket and blew, just like before dog appeared "hello boy" said Alfie making a big fuss of him, "it's great to see you again, it's been a while lets play". Alfie stood up to find a stick to throw for dog to fetch, but dog had ran off into the cave, "no dog", shouted Alfie "I don't have time to go on an adventure, but dog had gone so Alfie followed him into the cave to bring him back.

Once inside the cave Alfie realised he was outside again, there was miles and miles of grass, lots of trees and bushes and a large mass of water, suddenly he heard a noise behind him as Alfie turned around he could not believe his eyes it was a giraffe eating leaves of the top of the tree, he knew it was a giraffe because he had seen one before in London zoo when he went with his friends from school on a special trip. "You there, boy", a man shouted "have you lost a dog?" Alfie saw a man walking towards him with dog in his hands, "Yes I did thanks" said Alfie as he took dog from him. "My name is John" he said "I'm the gamekeeper here on the game reserve I protect the animals from poachers", he explained, "you seem to be lost son, I have my rounds to do now, would you and your dog like to join me, then I'll take you home", "yes please", said Alfie" that would be great", "ok then, jump into my jeep before the lions eat you", he said laughing.

The first place they came to was the water, Alfie was amazed at all the animals he could see, he felt that he was so close to them he would reach out his hand and touch them. There were hippopotamus's in the water keeping cool, elephants drinking water with their large trunks and zebra's eating grass beside the water and running by very fast were animals Alfie did not know, he turned to the gamekeeper and said "what are they sir?' "They are called gazelle's son have you never seen them before?" he asked "no sir not in London zoo," "ah I see, no they don't have gazelle's in London zoo, the animals would not survive living there". Alfie thought the gazelle's were really fast at running for such small animals, he loved watching them, "come lets try and find some lions for you to see", "lions" gasped Alfie, John just laughed "don't worry you will be fine" he said.

They drove slowly into a large open area and parked the jeep. "Watch and listen carefully" John said to Alfie. After a few minutes John turned to Alfie pointed and said "look over there", Alfie looked just in time to see a pack of lions chasing a gazelle that had wondered from its herd, luckily the gazelle was too fast this time for the lions to catch it, "they are lioness's", John explained "they are the one's that do all the hunting while the lions laze around all day in the shade look", and sure enough under the bushes Alfie could see the lazy lions. "Let me show you the wildebeest", said John "I am sure you do not have them in London zoo either". He turned the jeep around and drove further away from the water, "look there", he said pointing to a herd of huge animals, they looked like large bulls Alfie had seen in the fields he passed by on the train. "Wow", Alfie said " they are enormous and so many, do the lions eat them too" he asked "not very often", John replied "they are too large for the lioness's to kill".

"It's time to go back to the game reserve", John said to Alfie so he slowly turned his jeep around and headed back. The game reserve was surrounded by a high fence "that's to protect the animals we have in our care," John explained "the other animals can sense our animals are weak and would attack them for food, we nurse them better and when they are stronger we release them back into the wild, the baby elephant needs feeding would you like to do it?" he asked. "Yes please, said Alfie. John took Alfie to the pen where the baby elephant was, "her mother was killed by Poacher's", he explained "we are caring for her until she is old enough to care for herself". The baby elephant was beautiful and very playful she trod on poor Alfie's feet twice, "gosh" said Alfie "for a baby she is really heavy", john laughed "she certainly is", and handed Alfie the biggest bottle of milk he had ever seen, the baby elephant rushed over to Alfie, she was very hungry and drank the milk quickly until the bottle was empty, then fell fast asleep.

"Would you like to see the tiger cubs now" John asked. Alfie looked a bit worried "there's no need to worry the cubs are like puppies" he explained "oh yes please", said Alfie. John took Alfie to the pen where two tiger cubs were playing, he opened the gate and they went inside. John picked up one of the cubs and passed it to Alfie, he was right it was like holding a puppy, "just be careful", said john "they do have sharper teeth then a puppy'. Alfie sat on the floor playing with the tiger cubs, he was enjoying himself so much, he didn't hear dog barking from outside the pen, which told Alfie it was time to go. He thanked John the gamekeeper for the wonderful time, took out his penny whistle from his pocket and blew into it, once again Alfie found himself back inside the cave and dog was gone, he walked outside to the beach just in time to see his mother and uncle had arrived, he ran to her and gave her a big hug and she gave him a big kiss.

Back inside the lighthouse Alfie spent the day with his mother telling her all about the things he had done with uncle Thomas, he showed her his new coat and boots, "they are very smart Alfie" said his mother "but I am afraid you wont be needed them for school now". Alfie looked at his mother puzzled, "what do you mean mother", he asked. "I am sorry son" she explained "I do not have the room for you to stay with me anymore, the hospital is really busy and I have to share my room with two new nurses who are coming to work at the hospital, which means you cannot attend the school on the mainland. Uncle Thomas does not have time to bring you to the mainland everyday to go to school, I have spoken to the head teacher, we decided with their help your uncle Thomas will teach you at home, which he has agreed with."

Alfie felt sad, he was looking forward to having new friends to play with. "I have also some good news for you Alfie" his mother said, she could see he was upset, "do you remember Mrs Brown who lived next door to us in London? "Yes of cause I do mother" Alfie replied "I played with Bobby nearly everyday, (his real name was Robert but everyone called him Bobby). "Well", his mother continued "Mrs Brown wrote to me asking if there was room here in uncle Thomas's lighthouse for Bobby to stay, she is worried about the bombing in London and like us would prefer bobby to be safe living here, what do you think alfie? would you mind sharing your room with Bobby?, that would be wonderful mother", he said " I would love to share my room with Bobby, if uncle Thomas doesn't mind?. "I don't mind laddie" said uncle Thomas "I am going to be very busy soon with work and home schooling you and bobby, I am afraid I wont have a lot of time for playing so it is good you will have company of your own age, we can still play games in the evenings" he said smiling." Good that's settled then' said Alfie's mother "I will write to Mrs Brown straight away and tell her Bobby is welcome to stay".

After supper Alfie, his mother and uncle Thomas played games until bedtime, Alfie's mother was returning to the hospital tomorrow so Alfie was allowed to stay up later then usual, to make the most of the time he had with his mother. It was late so Alfie's mother took him up to bed and read him a story, "good night my darling", she said " you have a busy time ahead arranging your bedroom to make room for another bed, be extra good for uncle Thomas and be kind to bobby when he arrives he will be missing his home, but most of all have fun and I will be back to see you soon". She kissed him on the forehead and said goodnight then closed the bedroom door. In bed Alfie was thinking of all the fun times he will have playing with bobby, whom he could not wait to see again, then fell fast asleep.

CHAPTER 8

Bobby Comes To Stay

Alfie and his uncle Thomas had been busy getting Alfie's bedroom ready for the arrival of Bobby, Alfie's friend from London, who was coming to stay with them for a while, it had been a few weeks since Alfie's mother had visited and still bobby had not arrived, also Alfie's school holiday's were finished and uncle Thomas was now teaching Alfie at home.

When do you think Bobby will arrive?"Alfie asked his uncle, "are you bored with my company already laddie", he laughed. "No never" replied Alfie, "it's just that you have been really busy lately and it would be nice to have someone to play with". "I know laddie", said uncle "why don't you come with me today to the mainland, we can collect our post, maybe a letter will be waiting for us with good news?" "Ok uncle, " replied Alfie.

After lunch Alfie and his uncle left for the mainland. When they arrived uncle Thomas told Alfie to go to the post office to see if there were any letters or parcels for them while he brought the spare parts needed for the boat, "come straight back here I will be waiting for you" he said. Alfie ran off to the post office leaving uncle Thomas busy with supplies, he had just finished loading the boat when Alfie returned. 'I've got a letter for you uncle" he said passing the envelope to him. The letter was from London "it's from Mrs Brown Alfie" said uncle "your friend Bobby had caught chicken pox and that's why he is late coming, but he is all better now and will be arriving tomorrow, your mother will meet Bobby of the train and bring him to the port where we will be waiting for him", "hurray", said Alfie "I cant wait".

When they had reached home and packed everything away uncle Thomas told Alfie to make up the spare bed in his bedroom ready for his friend. Alfie was very excited he couldn't wait , it felt like such a long time since he had seen Bobby.

Uncle Thomas was busy on the beach replacing the spare parts on the boat, they were starting to get rusty from the sea water, so Alfie could not go on an adventure with his magic whistle today, his uncle would see him. Alfie was bored the day went very slowly, he even went to bed early after supper, he took his book to read and was soon fast asleep.

The next day Alfie and his uncle were waiting on the mainland for Alfie's mother to arrive at the port with Bobby.

"There they are" said Alfie as his mother and bobby arrived. "This is alfie's uncle Thomas" she said to Bobby, "hello laddie" said uncle Thomas, "welcome aboard my boat", "wow" said Bobby "are we really going to ride on the boat" he asked, "yes dear" answered Alfie's mother "Alfie will show you what to do" she then hugged Alfie and uncle Thomas goodbye and returned to the hospital.

Once on the boat alfie showed bobby how to put on the life jacket and told him to hold on tight to the rope. Bobby felt a little sick riding on the boat, he had never been on one before, especially one that went so fast. "Don't worry", said alfie "you will soon get use to it". When they had reached the lighthouse uncle Thomas told alfie to show bobby around the small island .

The boy's put Bobby's small suitcase in their bedroom then went to explore. First of all they climbed the rocks together, "wow, you can see right out into the ocean", said bobby to Alfie "I know isn't it terrific" Alfie replied. Next they walked down to the beach "have you swam in the sea alfie?" Bobby asked "oh yes" said Alfie "with my uncle, its too cold to swim now, you will have to wait until summer when its warmer", "that's ok I cant swim", bobby said sadly, "don't worry my uncle Thomas will teach you" Alfie replied, which made Bobby smile. As they walked along the beach Bobby noticed the cave, "gosh that looks scary", he said to Alfie "have you been inside?" "Yes, but it is not scary", he told Bobby of how he found the penny whistle, it was magical and how by going into the cave it took him on lots of adventures.

Alfie sat bobby down on the sand and began to tell him all about his magical adventures, the Funfair, being a page for the great red knight and going on safari to see all the wonderful animals and best of all dog. They had sat on the sand for a long time together talking until Alfie said, "you cant tell anyone what I have told you, it is a secret, I promise", said Bobby "if you show me?" "I will, " replied Alfie excitedly, just then uncle Thomas shouted to the boys, "lunch time lads and afterwards you have school work to do". "Ah" said Bobby, "don't worry", said Alfie, "we have plenty of time together for adventures, wait and see".

The boys did as uncle Thomas asked and straight after lunch they had lessons, it was too late in the afternoon for an adventure so they played board games together and talked of the good times they had playing together in London. Bobby told Alfie how scary it was when the bombs were dropped in London, "mostly at night time when I was asleep", he explained to Alfie, "my mother had to wake us to go to the air raid shelter, it was horrible, I was always tired", "your safe here now", said Alfie who was really pleased to have his friend with him.

After supper uncle told the boys he had to go the mainland first thing in the morning, "its an emergency", he explained, "I will be gone all day, will you be ok making your own lunch and possible supper, I have cold meat, boiled eggs and pickles in the fridge, have as much bread as you like, I will be back as soon as I can". "Don't worry uncle Thomas", said Alfie "we will be fine".

That night in bed the boys were thinking of what adventure they were to have the next day while uncle was away, "I hope its pirates", said Bobby, then fell asleep. It had been a long day for them both.

CHAPTER 9

The Circus

The boys woke up early the next day to have breakfast with Alfie's uncle Thomas before he left to go to the mainland, "make your beds and wash up the breakfast things please boys", said uncle Thomas, "be good, I will be back later this evening". "Ok", they both replied," then we can go to the beach", said Alfie to bobby, "it's a bit cold for the beach", replied Bobby, looking puzzled.

Alfie made the beds while Bobby washed the breakfast things, they then made their way to the beach, bobby turned to Alfie and said "What happens now?" Alfie took his penny whistle out of his pocket and blew, "there's no sound", said bobby until he heard barking, "it's a dog?" he said, "yes I know" replied Alfie, Bobby this is dog the one I told you about", dog jumped up to Bobby wagging his tail, "hello dog", he said stroking dogs head, I've never had a pet dog", said Bobby, "where's he going?" to the cave of cause", Alfie said "come on lets follow him".

Alfie and Bobby walked into the cave after dog and found themselves, standing in front of a very large red and white tent. "Wow, is that real", asked Bobby, "I've never been to a circus before", "come on lets go in", said Alfie.

The boys walked though the opening of the tent, then stood still in amazement, the tent was full of people waiting for the show to start. "Over here boys", shouted the man pointing to two seats right in the front row. Alfie and Bobby went and sat down, as they looked around them they saw they were sitting in front of a large circle with sawdust in the middle. Above their heads was a tight rope between two very tall stands and above the tight rope were two rope swings with a metal bar across tied to the stands.

On the other side opposite the boys was a small band, two men came in from the other side of the tent, sat down at the instruments and started playing, one played a drum and the other played the banjo. The audience started to clap as the ringmaster walked into the circle.
"Ladies and gentlemen, boys and girls we have a spectacular show for you today are you ready", shouted the ringmaster, and everyone cheered, "I cant here you", he shouted even louder, everyone cheered louder, "let the show begin, please put your hands together and clap really

loud for miss Susie and her performing seals". Miss Susie and her performing seals came into the ring, there were four seals all in a row, Miss Susie blew a whistle and all the seals waved to the audience, which made the children laugh and cheer, next she placed a small barrel on the ground and said, "up", one of the seals put its front flippers onto the barrel and rolled it across the ring, the audience clapped again, then Miss Susie threw a ball at each seal, which they caught by balancing them on their noses and at the same time clapped themselves with their flippers, they then bowed to the audience and waved goodbye as they left the ring.

Alfie and Bobby clapped and cheered the loudest. "That was amazing", Bobby whispered to Alfie, but before Afie could reply the ringmaster came back into the ring.
For my next act "he bellowed, "Please welcome the great almond". Everyone cheered and clapped as the great almond entered the ring, taking hold of five skittles he began to juggle, throwing the skittles high in the air, faster and faster the skittles span above his head. Next he picked up three chairs and started to juggle them high in the air, and last of all he started to juggle coloured balls, first with three, then the ringmaster threw to him two more balls so there were five, then three more were thrown to him making eight altogether, high in the air the great almond juggled the balls catching them as they came back down, everyone clapped as he caught each ball one at a time, he then bowed to the audience and left the ring.

The ringmaster then shouted again "ladies and gentlemen, boys and girls the clowns". Three men came into the ring dressed in bright clothes with funny painted faces and red noses. They tumbled to the floor pretending to fall, which made the children laugh, then one took a plastic fish out of his pocket and slapped the other clowns in the face with it, making the clowns fall down again, the children laughed especially Alfie and Bobby, and because the children were laughing the clowns picked up buckets of water to throw at them, they pretended to throw the water over the children, over and over again making the children scream, which made the adults laugh and in the end the clowns did throw the water over the children but the buckets were only filled with tissue paper and ribbons making the children scream and laugh at the same time.

As the clowns left the ring, the ringmaster told the audience they were stopping for a break, but there was hotdogs and drinks for everyone. While Alfie and Bobby sat eating their hotdogs they chatted together about which act they liked the best, "I liked the seals" said Alfie, "yes I liked the great almond the juggler", replied Bobby, but they both agreed the clowns were the best. After they had finished their hotdogs and drank their drinks the show started again.

"A big cheer for Marcus the lion tamer", the ringmaster said, as the lights went back on the boys saw a cage had been placed in the middle of the ring and two lions were inside, with them was Marcus the lion tamer. The audience gasped with fright, but when Marcus cracked his whip the lions climbed onto boxes, the audience cheered. Marcus cracked his whip again and the lions sat up on their hind legs keeping their backs straight, again Marcus cracked his whip and the lions jumped off the boxes and lay down on the floor. Marcus then to everyone's surprise stepped over the lions one by one, everyone clapped really loud, Marcus then cracked his whip again, this time only one lion sat up and opened it's mouth, Marcus then placed his head inside the lions mouth, the audience gasped then went very quiet as Marcus took his head out of the lions mouth, then bowed to the audience, everyone clapped and cheered, "that was scary" said Alfie to Bobby, as the lion tamer and caged lions left the ring.

The ringmaster came back into the ring and said, "ladies and gentlemen, boys and girls please welcome the last act of the day, the flying Ronaldo's," pointing up above his head. Everyone looked up, high above their heads were a family on the large stands, a father, mother, son and daughter act. The mother began to slowly walk across the tightrope, which was held between the two large stands, balancing by holding a long pole, while she walked. The audience went completely quiet as they watched her high above their heads. Next the daughter followed her mother across the tightrope, the audience gasped as the young girl slightly lost her balance but managed to stay on, when she reached the other end everyone clapped and cheered. Next they watched the father and son climb higher above the tightrope to where the swings were. The father climbed onto the swing, untied it and swung to the middle, he then turned himself upside down on the swing, his legs held tight as his arms and head were tangling underneath as the swing moved back and forth. The son then untied the other swing held it with both hands and swung towards his father on the other swing, the boy let go of his swing and spun in a circle, and his father caught him by his feet, they were both swinging together, then the father let go of his son's feet and the boy grabbed hold of his swing again and swung back to the stand. Everyone one clapped and cheered really loud, "I've never seen anything like that before", said Alfie to Bobby, "I know it was fantastic', replied Bobby.

When the flying Ronaldo's came back down from the high stands the audience stood up to clap and cheer for them again, they all knew how dangerous their act was and thought it was wonderful.

Sadly the circus had finished, when the boys, left the circus tent dog was waiting for them. "I know dog", said Alfie "it's time to go", he took out his penny whistle from his trouser pocket and blew, the circus disappeared and they were back in the cave. They slowly walked back along the beach with dog, and then he was gone too.

When they returned to the lighthouse it was late and had began to get dark, they laid the table with the cold meat, boiled eggs, bread and pickles for their supper, they boys sat down and ate. It had been a long day and they both were hungry. "Thank you for bringing me with you on your magical adventure', Bobby said to Alfie, "I had a terrific time". Alfie smiled it was wonderful having magical adventures, but even more wonderful having someone to share them with. The boys chatted about the amazing circus until uncle Thomas came home.

CHAPTER 10

Halloween

Bobby had been staying in the lighthouse with Alfie and his uncle Thomas for quite a while now, he really enjoyed being there with them both, he liked Alfie's uncle Thomas very much and having Alfie to play with every day, he even didn't mind having to do school work every day.

This morning the boys were going over to the mainland with uncle Thomas to collect more supplies and the post, uncle Thomas had been too busy to go for a few weeks, he was painting and cleaning the lighthouse and maintaining the light at the top, "have to keep it shining brightly for our ships", he explained to the boys. Alfie was especially looking forward in going today because they were to meet his mother and go to the picture house to watch a film while uncle Thomas collected the supplies and post, afterwards they were going to the café for lunch as a treat. Bobby was not keen having to go on the boat again, he remembered how sick he felt last time he went on, but this time he was ok and actually began to enjoy the trip.

When they arrived Alfie's mother was waiting for them, she gave them all a hug as they got off the boat, "it's lovely to see you all, how are you settling in Bobby", she asked. "I love living at the lighthouse with Alfie and uncle Thomas," Bobby said smiling, I am pleased, replied Alfie's mother. Are you ready to go boys the picture starts soon and we have to walk there". They said goodbye to uncle Thomas and set off towards the picture house, they were going to see a Tarzan film. The picture house was full with boys and girls with their mothers waiting for the film to start, "these are our seats," said Aflie's mother, the boys settled down into their seats just as the curtain went back and the film began. Alfie's mother brought some sweets earlier for them to share, "oh thank you ", said Bobby popping one in his mouth.

The boys were quiet all the way through the film until the end. Alfie and bobby thanked his mother as they got up to leave, "that was brilliant", Alfie said to Bobby, "wouldn't it be great to have an adventure like Tarzan".

As they entered the café uncle Thomas was waiting for them, "I have saved these seats for us", he said, once they were seated the waitress came over and asked what would they like, "a pot of tea for two, two glasses of milk and crumpets with jam please", replied his mother. The boys ate their crumpets and drank their milk, while telling uncle Thomas all about the film, "it sounds like you had a great time boys", "I have another treat for you when we get back to the lighthouse, as its Halloween how would you like to camp outside tonight in a tent? He asked, "my friend at the port has lent us his tent, yes please", they both replied together. After lunch they said goodbye to Alfie's mother, who had to return to the hospital and walked back to the boat.

They returned to the lighthouse, the boys helped uncle Thomas unload the supplies and put them away. "I forgot Bobby you have a letter from your mother", uncle Thomas said handing the letter to Bobby, "sit down and read what she has to say while Alfie and I put up the tent".

Alfie enjoyed helping uncle Thomas put the tent up, it was just big enough for two people, "not too far from the lighthouse', said uncle Thomas, "the grass is nice and soft here". Alfie just finished banging in the last tent peg into the ground when Bobby came out to help. "What did your mother say laddie", asked uncle Thomas, "she said everyone back home was fine, but Nanna's cat got lost in an air raid and was found in next door's shed, and also how much she was missing me". Bobby felt terrible that his mother was missing him when he was having such a nice time, he soon felt better when he saw the tent was ready for them. "Wow that looks great", he said to Alfie and uncle Thomas. "I'll go and get the sleeping bags and the torches". They placed the sleeping bags inside the tent, "let me check the torches are working", said uncle Thomas and took them inside the lighthouse. Uncle Thomas checked the batteries, the torches were working fine, he placed them inside a small rack sack with a bottle of water, a few sweets and two comics, ready to give to the boys after supper. The boys helped to get supper ready and cleared the plates away when they had finished. "Don't worry boys I will do the washing up", said uncle Thomas, "you two go and get ready for bed, remember to put your jumpers back on over your pyjamas as it will get colder during the night". The boys raced upstairs to get ready they couldn't wait to go inside the tent. "Here are your torches and a few things", uncle Thomas said while passing the rack sack to Alfie, "have a great time boys and I will see you in the morning".

The boys went outside in the dark using their torches to see, they climbed inside the tent, took off their boots and placed them outside the tent, then zipped it up to keep the cold out, but kept their socks on in case they need to go to the toilet in the middle of the night, they didn't want to get their feet cold. They found the comics and sweets uncle Thomas had given them, "yippee", shouted Bobby, "I haven't read this one". The boys sat for a long time using their torches quietly reading their comics and eating the sweets, until Bobby said "I'm bored, and not tired yet what shall we do now"? "How about doing this", Alfie said as he took his penny whistle out from under his sleeping bag, he had hidden it there earlier when uncle Thomas was busy cooking their supper.

The boys quickly put their boots back on, picked up their torches and walked down to the beach, Alfie blew into his whistle, they heard dog barking but couldn't see him until they shone their torches on him. "There you are dog," said Alfie, "sorry we couldn't see you in the dark, that's because he's small", said Bobby. After making a fuss of dog, Alfie said, "you better follow us into the cave dog our torches will show us the way". As they walked inside the cave they realised it was still dark, using their torches they could see a large house surrounded by a graveyard. "I don't like the look of that", said Bobby, "lets go back, don't be such a scaredy cat", said Alfie, "come on we have dog here with us".

The boys slowly walked past the large iron gates into the graveyard, "there's a path here", said Alfie "lets follow it". Suddenly there was a strange noise, "what was that?" Bobby whispered, Alfie shone the torch where the noise came from, "look its only an owl", he said shining his torch high up towards a tree, "come on", they slowly carried on walking, just as a black cat jumped out at them onto the path, it screeched loudly as it came across dog who started barking, which chased the cat away, both boys started to laugh, "silly cat", said Bobby. The boys carried on walking, "look", said Alfie to Bobby pointing his torch high in the trees as they walked passed them there were paper skeletons and ghosts hanging down from them, as the boys turned the corner they saw more paper skeletons hanging from some of the graves. "This is great", Alfie said to Bobby, as they got closer to the large house, they could see it was completely pitch black, not one light shining. "Don't you think its time to go home", said Bobby getting scared again, "we're nearly there", said Alfie, "lets just take a quick look".

As the boys reached the front door of the large house, a man jumped out dressed in a ghost costume, shouting happy Halloween, Alfie and Bobby both screamed, "gosh I am sorry," said the man, "I didn't mean to frighten you, only to play a trick on you, my name is William and this is my home, please come in". William opened the door so the boys could see lights on all over the house and a warm fire glowing, "come and warm yourselves by the fire", he said, "while I make some hot chocolate". The boys sat down on the comfy chairs in front of the fire, while dog lay down on the rug. "Here you are boys", said William passing them the hot drink, I hope you like toasted marshmallows". "My name is Alfie and this is Bobby and dog", said Alfie. "Very nice to meet you all", replied William. While the marshmallows were toasting in the fire

William told the boys how he had travelled all over the world mostly by train, which was his favourite way to travel, and all the amazing things he had seen, the great wall of china and the Grand Canyon, how he flew an aeroplane across to France and when he sailed on a large ship and much more. They chatted and chatted until dog started to bark, "gosh sir", said Alfie "we have to go now, thank you very much for the hot chocolate and marshmallows, you're very welcome boys". Said William, "its been lovely to meet you both". As they waved goodbye Alfie took his whistle out of his pocket and blew, once again they were back in the cave and dog had gone. "I'm really tired now", said Bobby as they walked back to the tent, once inside they climbed into their sleeping bags and fell fast asleep.

CHAPTER 11

The Wild West

The next morning the boys woke up cold, with their sleeping bags wrapped around them they quickly went back inside the lighthouse where uncle Thomas was waiting for them, "here you are boys", he said " a lovely mug of hot milk for you both, thanks uncle Thomas", they both replied, they sat down at the table to drink their milk and eat the bread and jam he had made for their breakfast. "Did you have fun sleeping in the tent last night", he asked the boys, "Yes thank you " they both replied " and thank you for the sweets and comics".

After breakfast the boys got dressed and helped uncle Thomas to take the tent down ready to be returned to his friend on the mainland. They then had school lessons to do, "when you have finished your lessons Bobby why don't you write a nice letter to your mother, she would like that very much, ok ", replied Bobby. The boys were busy all morning studying until there was a knock at the door, which was very unusual, they didn't have many visitors. Uncle Thomas answered the door to find his friend had come across from the mainland on his boat, he had brought a very important message for uncle Thomas, "one of our ships is slowly sinking", uncle Thomas explained to the boys, "all boats are needed to rescue the crew aboard the ship, I am to go straight away with Mr Jones to help, you boys will have to make your own lunch again sorry and don't forget to write your letter to your mother Bobby", he said as he was leaving.
The boys thought it sounded ever so exciting to rescue the crew on a war ship, " we better do as uncle Thomas asked", said Alfie to Bobby, "I'll make us sandwiches for lunch while you write your letter to your mother".

Bobby finished writing his letter to his mother, then had the jam sandwiches Alfie had made for their lunch, after washing up the dishes they sat down to read the pages in the book uncle Thomas had left for them as part of their school lessons. "I'm bored", said Bobby, "can we try your magic whistle again Alfie? " ok " replied alfie, " uncle Thomas wont be back for a long time and we have finished our reading".

They put their coats on and walked down to the beach, Alfie blew into his penny whistle and dog appeared "good boy ", Bobby said shaking his paw and patting dog on the head, "come on lets go." Said Bobby. The boys chased dog onto the cave where they found themselves out in the open, as they looked around they saw huge rock caves, prickly cactuses and dusty sand everywhere, just then a man on a large wagon driven by a horse came down the dusty road, he was dressed in jeans, a coloured shirt, boots and a large cowboy hat on his head. "Howdy boys do you need a lift into town?" he asked. "Yes please", the boys replied, "then jump in the back of the wagon", the cowboy said, then shouted to his horse giddy up and away they went. "Your not from around here", said the cowboy, "no, we are just visiting", replied Alfie. Bobby noticed the cowboy had a gun and said, "Is that a real gun mister? It sure is, 'the cowboy replied 'have you boys never used a gun before?" he asked, "no sir", said Alfie, "then I will have to show you how", he replied, "whoa", the cowboy shouted to the horse to make it stop, "come down and I'll show you how to shoot with a gun". The boys excitedly got off the wagon and followed the cowboy, who had placed three old tin cans on a rock in front of them. "Who wants to be first", he asked the boys. "I will", said Bobby. The cowboy took his hand gun out of his holster and stood behind Bobby, he placed his gun in Bobby's right hand, placing his finger on the trigger of the gun, "put your arm up straight, keep your eye level with the tin cans", he explained, "take aim, pull back the trigger and fire". "BANG", the gun went off really loudly, which made the boys jump, Bobby missed the tin cans, "don't worry son", said the cowboy smiling, "try again, but this time level the gun with the tin cans by using both of your eyes', Bobby did as he was told, "BANG" the gun went again but this time Bobby shot the tin can off the rock. "Hurray", the boys cheered, "well done son", said the cowboy, patting Bobby on the back, it was Alfie's turn. Standing quite still Alfie aimed the gun, "BANG", went the gun shooting the tin can off the rock. "Hurray", the boys cheered again. Both boys had great fun learning to shoot a gun and thanked the cowboy, thanks mister", they said, "it was brilliant".

They all got back onto the wagon and headed towards town. "Here you are boys", said the cowboy, the boys jumped down of the wagon and said goodbye to the cowboy.

The town looked just like the boys had seen in a western film at the picture house, there was a saloon, which they knew was where the cowboys went for a drink, on the other side of the town was a jail house with bars, as they looked inside the jail the boys saw a cowboy locked up inside, "gosh", said Alfie to Bobby, "he must be a robber", as they were looking inside another cowboy came out of the jail house and said, "off with you, this is no place for you", the boys noticed he was wearing a sheriff badge, "sorry sir", the boys said and quickly moved away. "Wow a Sheriff", said Bobby to Alfie.

They carried on walking through the town looking at all the stores, one sold food supplies and clothes, mainly jeans and cowboy hats. A man in a white apron came out of the store, turned to the boys and said "you there would you deliver these goods for me, my lad has hurt his foot and is unable to do his rounds today, I will pay you for your help". "Sure thing mister", the boys replied and set off with the goods and a list of where they were to be taken. The first store for a delivery was the barber who cut hair and shaved beards, next was the store that sold guns, lots and lots of guns, the boys stopped for a while to have a look through the window, there were guns the same as the cowboy had when he showed the boys how to shoot, guns in holsters and large rifles, which you needed both hands to hold when you shoot.

The boys had never seen so many gun's they spent some time looking though the window in amazement. The next delivery was for the hotel which was further done the street, as they arrived at the hotel a stage coach stopped to let passengers off, the owner of the hotel was already outside helping the passengers with their luggage, he told the boys to leave the box of deliveries on the ground beside him, which he proceeded to pick up and carry into the hotel.

The last delivery was for the stables at the end of the town. The stables were full of horses and cows, a boy of the same age as Alfie and Bobby called to them to place the delivery down beside the stables. Alfie and Bobby did as they were asked placing the box down on the ground. The boy was playing with a rope trying to throw it over a tree trunk, the boys stood watching as he managed to catch the rope over the tree truck at every throw. "Wow" said Alfie that's really clever. "Have you never lasso with a rope before", the boy asked, "no never" replied Alfie and Bobby together. "Well I will have to show you how, my name is Jake", he said, "my name is Alfie and this is my friend Bobby, Alfie replied, "it would be great if you could show us how to lasso a rope". Jake explained to Alfie and Bobby that first they take one end of the rope and make a large circle, then tie it loosely, that is called a lasso, but first you spin the rope above your head, then throw it at the object you are trying to lasso, once you catch the lasso around it, you pull hard to tighten the rope, it is a lot harder when the object is moving like cattle and not still like this old tree trunk". Alfie and Bobby both decided to have a go at lassoing the tree trunk, Alfie tried first, he stood in front of the tree trunk and began spinning the rope above his head, he then threw the rope at the tree trunk and sadly missed. "Try again", said Jake. Alfie tried and missed again and again and again. "Gosh this is hard". He said to Bobby "you try", so Bobby did and like Alfie he too missed the tree trunk again and again and again. "It is very difficult to do ", explained Jake, "I have been practicing since I was five years old". "Never mind ", said Alfie , "it was fun trying". The boys thanked Jake for showing them how to lasso a rope and left to return to the store where the man with the white apron was waiting for them. "All goods delivered", said Alfie to the man, "well done boys and thank you for your help, here are two cowboy hats for your payment". The man put the red hat on top of Bobby's head and the black hat on top of Alfie's head, "have a look in the mirror boys, you look like real cowboys now", he said and they did.

Alfie and bobby thanked the man and left the store to join dog, outside waiting for them. "Time to go home", Alfie said to Bobby and blew into his whistle. They were back in the cave and dog was gone, but to their surprise they were still wearing their cowboy hats the man had given them. Happily they walked back along the beach chatting about the great adventure in the wild west they had, when they saw uncle Thomas's boat making its way back to shore. "Lets run back to the lighthouse and put our cowboy hats away, then make supper for uncle Thomas," Alfie said to Bobby, "I am sure uncle will be very tired.

Uncle Thomas walked into the lighthouse and saw bobby setting the table and Alfie making supper, "hot soup and bread for supper," said Alfie, "that's grand boys, thank you," uncle replied sitting down by the fire, "and how was your day boys", he asked, "I hope you had fun?" The boys looked at each other and smiled, "yes we had lots of fun", they replied," suppers ready", said Alfie. They sat down together at the table and ate. After they cleared away the supper things and sat down in front of the warm fire listening to the wireless, "early to bed boys," said uncle Thomas, "I am worn out tonight'.

They all said goodnight and went to bed

CHAPTER 12

Guy Fawkes Night

Alfie and Bobby had been busy helping uncle Thomas in the lighthouse, they helped fix the shutters across the windows, they helped mend the water pipe, and they helped chop up the old furniture that had broken for the fire. Today uncle Thomas sent the boys down to the beach to shovel sand into sacks, placing the sacks onto the wheel barrow ready to wheel back up to the lighthouse it was really hard work, which took the boys all morning. "Why do we need sand uncle", Alfie asked, sitting down to lunch, "to spread on the path when it becomes icy "he replied.

It was now November and the weather was getting colder and colder. Uncle Thomas had placed a heavy curtain across the front door, "its to keep the cold out", he explained, he then placed a shovel by the front door, "what is the shovel for?" asked Bobby "to shovel the snow of the path when it comes, so we can get out of the door", replied uncle Thomas.

It was Guy Fawkes the 5th of November tomorrow and the boys were disappointed because they couldn't build a bonfire or have any fireworks. "I am sorry boys ", said uncle Thomas, "its against the law to have a bonfire glowing or fireworks lighting up the sky, the glare from them both would be strong enough for German aeroplanes to spot, they would drop bombs on us", he explained. "Cheer up boys I have a little surprise for you both tomorrow. What is it?" asked Bobby, "just wait and see laddie", uncle Thomas replied.

That night tucked up warm in their beds the boys couldn't sleep, "I wonder what surprise uncle Thomas has for us", said Alfie, "I don't know what it could be?" replied Bobby, "maybe it has something to do with your mother coming to stay tomorrow?" After exchanging different ideas to each other of what the surprise might be, they both finally fell asleep.

The next morning after breakfast uncle Thomas left to collect Alfie's mother from the mainland, who was coming to stay, leaving Alfie and Bobby painting the window shutters they had helped uncle Thomas to fix yesterday. When Alfie's mother arrived she was carrying a small cardboard box with her, after giving the boys a hug she handed them some sweets she had brought for them, saying thank you the boys sat down to eat them. "What's in the cardboard box mother ", Alfie asked, "a surprise for you both ", she replied, "but first of tell me what you have been doing since I last saw you?" The boys told her of the fun they had sleeping in the tent on Halloween night, "but it was awfully cold when we woke up in the morning", said Bobby, "yes but uncle Thomas made us hot milk to warm us up", said Alfie. They sat down at the table for lunch chatting more while they ate.

After lunch they went for a walk around the island, making sure to wrap up warm, Alfie had his new coat to wear, which he felt very smart in. They collected some old wood, which had drifted onto the beach from the sea for the open fire as they walked. "It is so beautiful here, I do love coming to stay, especially when I can get lots of kisses from my two favourite boys", Alfie's mother said laughing as she chased the boys trying to catch them, who had ran away quickly so not to be kissed.

When they returned to the lighthouse they took off their shoes and hung up their coats, mother said they could now see what she had brought with her in the cardboard box. She placed the box on the table for the boys to open it, slowly they took out things that were inside and placed them on the table to have a look, there was four long metal forks, eight sausages and rolls and a packet of marshmallows to eat and for a real treat a bottle of cola. "Hurray" the boys shouted, "there's more", said Alfie's mother, she put her hand inside the box and pulled out a box of indoor fireworks. The boys screeched with delight, "but uncle Thomas said we couldn't have fireworks", said Alfie to his mother, they are indoor fireworks laddie", explained uncle Thomas, "to use inside the house only, they cannot be seen from the outside, now off upstairs both of you and make a small guy to put on the fire".

The boys raced upstairs to their bedroom to make a guy, they sat down on the bedroom floor together, first by using old rags and one of uncle Thomas's old socks they began to make a guy. They filled the old sock with rags, then tied the end with a piece of string, taking another piece of string they tied it around the top of the sock to make a small head, "its beginning to look like a guy already", said Bobby. With pencils and paper they drew two arms, two legs and a round smiley face, then carefully cutting out the drawings they glued them onto the sock. First they glued the face on and then the arms and legs. "Finished", Alfie said taking the guy downstairs to show his uncle and mother. "That's wonderful boys", said Alfie's mother and uncle, "now go and wash your hands, you are going to cook your own sausages".

The boys washed their hands at the sink in the kitchen, while Alfie's mother placed a sausage on the end of the long forks, while uncle Thomas placed four chairs in front of the fire ready for them to sit on. Once everyone was seated, Alfie's mother passed them a fork each, "place the fork over the fire like this", she explained to the boys showing them what to do," your sausages will slowly cook". What fun the boys were having cooking their own sausages over the fire. When they were ready to eat Alfie's mother placed them inside the rolls with tomato ketchup poured on top, " yummy" they said as she passed the plates.

They sat happily eating their sausage rolls, chatting, laughing and drinking their cola, Bobby turned to Alfie's mother and said, "can I have another one please, of cause you can, ' she replied placing another sausage each on the end of the forks. When they had finished eating Alfie's mother washed up the plates while uncle Thomas prepared the indoor fireworks.

Uncle Thomas placed a plate on the kitchen table then placed a firework in the middle of the plate, the firework was made of lightweight paper, when uncle Thomas lit it with his matches the paper burned forming a shape like a wriggly snake, "wow", said the boys, "that's amazing, he then lit another firework, it blew into the air, then burnt out, "hurray", shouted the boys, "do another one please", they said. It was magical watching the paper fireworks floating above their heads and watching the different shapes they made each time they were lit, until the box was empty. The boys hugged Alfie's mother to say thank you for their lovely surprise and gave her a kiss on her cheek.

They then all sat back down together in front of the fire toasting their marshmallows while uncle Thomas told scary stories until bedtime, which made them all laugh.

CHAPTER 13

Buckingham Palace

Alfie's mother was going back to the hospital on the mainland today, where she worked as a nurse. The boys had a wonderful time having her to play with, they played cards, board games and hide and seek, but most of all they loved the stories she read to them at bedtime. But it was time to go, she hugged the boys goodbye and said, "I will be back soon, be good for uncle Thomas", as they waved goodbye Bobby felt very sad, "I really miss my mother", he said to alfie,"cheer up", said Alfie,"it will be Christmas soon and you will be going home".

Bobby's mother had written to uncle Thomas to tell him he was to return home for Christmas as she was missing him and longed to see him, it had been such a long time, they were going to stay at his auntie's house, his home had sadly been bombed by German aeroplanes and his mother was now living with his auntie. Bobby was looking forward in seeing his mother again, but he was going to miss Alfie and uncle Thomas very much.

"I know how to cheer you up", said Alfie, "lets go on an adventure, uncle Thomas will be away most of the day, come on it might be the last time we can go together, before you leave". "Ok", said Bobby and ran back into the lighthouse to fetch the penny whistle.

"Are you ready ", said Alfie to Bobby and blew into his whistle. Dog appeared jumping up at them licking their faces, "good boy", said Bobby wiping his face, " lets go". They ran to the cave, as they entered, they found themselves inside a very large hall with huge pillars and a staircase that seem to go all the way to the top of the house, suddenly a man shouted, "you boys you are not allowed in here, go back down to the servants quarters, pointing to another staircase behind them. Alfie and Bobby did as they were told and started to make their way down the stairs, as they reached the bottom a girl came up to them, "hello', she said, "who are you?" My name is Alfie and my name is Bobby", they replied, "my name is Daisy, I live here with my father, he is the butler to King George and Queen Elizabeth". "Where are we", the boys gasped", why in Buckingham Palace of cause", she replied, "come on lets play". Daisy took the boys back up the stairs, quickly hiding behind a pillar from the man the boys had met earlier, "that's Arthur", said Daisy, "he doesn't like me playing up here". They hurried up the stairs into some rooms, then up some more stairs, until daisy turned to them and said, "here we are", she opened the doors of a huge room, then they entered inside.

Alfie and Bobby could not believe their eyes they were standing in what looked like a huge toy shop, dolls houses, a rocking horse, a huge train set, teddies, dolls and much more. "This is the nursery where the princesses play", explained Daisy. "Are we allowed in here", Alfie asked, "I always come here to play when the princesses are away", Daisy explained, "away?" said Bobby, 'yes they have gone to stay in Winsor Castle, so we are quite safe to be here, Arthur never comes up here".

The children began to play with the toys daisy went straight to the dolls house to play with, which was her favourite. Bobby jumped onto the rocking horse shouting "giddy up cowboy", as he rocked the horse faster and faster, and Alfie played with the train set. The train set had a station like the one Alfie saw with his mother the day they came to stay with uncle Thomas, and a light signal, which he moved with his hand, red for stop, green for go, "whoa whoa", said Alfie mimicking the noise of a train as he pushed it around the track. "That looks like fun", said Bobby 'can I play too? Of cause you can", said Alfie, "its more fun with two".

The boys happily played with the train set for a long time, until Daisy said "I'm getting hungry, would you boys like something to eat?" "Yes please", they replied. The children made their way back down the stairs to the kitchen, where the cook was busy making sandwiches for all the staff, "there you are Daisy", she said, "and you have some friends with you today, sit down loves and I'll get you a glass of milk each", as she passed them a plate of sandwiches to eat, "thanks missus" said the boys as they ate.

After they had finished eating Daisy asked if they would like to see the guards, they were outside practising their marching. "Yes please", the boys said, "that would be great to see". They followed Daisy to another large room at the back of the palace, "this is the best window to look out from", explained Daisy. The boys stood at the large window with daisy watching the guards march. "Look at their funny hats", said Bobby, "their called bearskins", explained Daisy, "their amazing", said Alfie, as he watched the guards marching in line up and down the courtyard, changing direction when the officer in charge shouted his instructions. The children watched the guards until Bobby said, "I'm bored now can we go and play?" "I know ", said Daisy "lets go outside in the gardens and pretend to march like the guards".

The boys thought that was a great idea and followed Daisy through the large hall, back down the stairs to the kitchen and out the back door that led to the gardens. "Can I be leader", asked Alfie. Leading the children they marched all around the gardens, in and out of the arches, around the large fountain and across the wall. "Lets play hide and seek now", said Daisy. "I'll count to fifty and you hide", 1234. Daisy started to count as the boys ran off to hide. "Ready or not here I come", she shouted.

Daisy ran to the bushes but no one was hiding there, she then ran to the large tree, but no one was hiding there either, where can they be she thought to herself, then she tried over the wall, "found you ", she said to Alfie who was hiding there. "Ah you found me", said Alfie a little disappointed to be found first. "Come on lets look for Bobby together", said Daisy.

They searched all over the gardens until finally behind the large fountain daisy shouts, "I've found you", "ah ", Bobby moaned, "it was the best hiding place, you took a ling time to fine me?" The children laughed, suddenly dog appeared and started to bark, "a dog", said Daisy. "Where did he come from?" "He's our dog " explained Alfie, "he has been waiting here for us". "Can I play with him", asked Daisy. Dog jumped up and licked Daisy's face, "he likes you", said Bobby, "come on lets play chase", said Daisy then ran down the garden with dog chasing her, laughing and laughing she ran around in circles, while dog chased her, she then picked up a stick and threw it for dog to fetch, "good boy", she said when dog brought the stick back for her to throw again and again.

"We have to go now", said Alfie, "oh, thank you for playing with me today", replied Daisy, "I've had a wonderful time, I hope you come and play again sometime", she said as she waved goodbye and ran back inside the palace.

Alfie took his whistle from out of his pocket and blew, once again the boys were back inside the cave and dog was gone.
As they arrived back at the lighthouse uncle Thomas came through the front door. "I'm home boys, "I hope you haven't been too bored without me, after supper we can play a board game of your choice, what will it be? He asked, "Monopoly", they shouted together and laughed.

CHAPTER 14

Shopping For Christmas

The weeks had gone by quickly and Bobby was to go home tomorrow. Alfie was very quiet after breakfast, he loved having bobby to play with everyday and he was going to miss him terribly. "Cheer up laddie", said uncle Thomas, "Bobby will back next year, and we have Christmas to look forward to, I know", he said "would you boys like to go to the mainland today to buy Christmas presents?" "Yes please uncle Thomas, they both replied. "I would like to buy something nice for my mother", said Bobby "What about you Alfie?" uncle asked "I would like to buy something for mother and father", he replied. Alfie had not seen his father now for nearly a year, he was fighting in the war. Alfie's mother too had not been able to visit since the last time she stayed was in November, that was seven weeks ago, she had sent a letter to uncle Thomas to explain there had been an emergency at the hospital and unable to see them for a while, uncle Thomas knew what was happening but he promised Alfie's mother not say anything to the boys.

The boys grabbed their coats and made their way down to the boat, uncle Thomas was busy pulling the heavy cover of it that keeps the boat dry during winter. "Hop aboard boys", he said, "we will be leaving soon". The crossing on the sea was choppy which made the boat sway up and down more, poor Bobby felt sick again.

When they had reached the mainland uncle Thomas handed the boys some money, not much, just enough to get something nice for their parents. "Off you go boys", meet me back here in two hours, I have some Christmas shopping to do of my own" " he said winking with his eye. The boys thanked uncle Thomas and ran of to the shops. "We can keep an eye on the time from the old clock at the post office", Alfie said to Bobby, as they entered the first shop to have a look around.

The shop sold lots of different things, pocket watches, fountain pens, silk scarf's and much more. "Wow", said Bobby, as he picked up a penknife, "look at this, I don't think your mother would like one of those", said Alfie, so Bobby put the penknife back. "What about a silk scarf", asked Bobby, "yes your mother would like one of those", Alfie replied, but when Bobby looked at the price, the cost of the scarf was two much money he had to spend. "Never mind", said Alfie, "there are plenty of other shops to look around".

The boys left the shop and went to the sweet shop, "we could buy a box of chocolates for our mothers", said Alfie, "yes but they wont last forever", said Bobby, 'then the present is gone", he explained. So the boys left the sweet shop to try somewhere else.

They came to a shop with pictures in photo frames at the window for people to look at, "lets try in here", said Alfie.

Inside the shop were photo frames of all shapes and sizes in lots of different patterns and colours. The boys looked around the shop in amazement, "look at this one", said Bobby as he picked up a small frame made of wood with a red rose painted on it, "my mother loves roses", said Bobby, "do you think your uncle Thomas would let me have the picture he took of me with his camera, so I can put it inside the frame for my mother as a surprise", he asked Alfie, "yes I'm sure he will", Alfie replied. Bobby took the frame to the counter and asked the lady how much the frame was, Bobby was so pleased when he realised he had enough money to buy the frame and some left over to get uncle Thomas a gift for letting him stay with them. The lady placed the frame inside a small box, Bobby paid her the correct money and thanked her. "That just leaves you to find something for your mother and father", said Bobby, but Alfie was still not sure of what to buy, he wanted something really special but could not think of anything. "Lets go next door into the café and have a drink, while we try and think of something", suggested Bobby. The boys sat down inside the café and ordered a cola with two straws for them to share. They both sat quietly trying hard to think of a gift for Alfie's parents. Alfie wanted to buy something he could send to his father to keep with him always. "It has to be something small to keep inside his uniform pocket", he explained to Bobby. They sat for a long time thinking while drinking their cola, but still both boys could not come up with an idea of what to buy.

They left the café and walked towards the post office to check the time as they had been shopping for quite a while, just as they turned into the street where the post office was they saw on the corner a shop with two small teddy bears in the shop window, one with a blue scarf tied around the neck and the other with a pink scarf, "that's it", shouted Alfie pointing at the shop window, "perfect", he said to Bobby "matching small teddy bears, one each for mother and father to keep with them always, to remind them of me when they felt lonely". The boys went inside the shop to buy the teddies, the lady in the shop smiled when Alfie told her what the teddies were for, she kindly placed each teddy inside a box, "oh thank you very much", said Alfie as he gave the lady the money.

The boys were so pleased with their gifts for their parents and even more pleased they had enough money left to buy uncle Thomas the penknife they had seen in the first shop they went into. They entered the shop again and told the man behind the counter the penknife they wanted for their uncle because his penknife was old and the blade was wearing away. The man wrapped the penknife safely away they thanked the man, then left the shop to walk back to the boat.

When they had reached the boat uncle Thomas was waiting for them with a surprise, he had brought a Christmas tree for the boys to decorate when they return to the lighthouse, and then it started to snow.

When they returned home uncle Thomas placed the Christmas tree in a bucket full of sand and brought it inside the lighthouse for the boys to decorate with the old decorations uncle Thomas had kept since he was a boy.
"We have finished decorating the tree uncle Thomas", said Alfie, he came out of his back room to have a look "that's a grand job you have done boys"; he said as he past them two presents to place under the tree, to the boys surprise the presents had their names on, "hurray", said Bobby "I cant wait to open mine, you can open yours tomorrow morning before you leave", said uncle Thomas to Bobby, "now be of with you and play, go and look outside the window boys", to their amazement the snow had settled very quickly, "come on lets go", said Alfie to Bobby, they ran upstairs to put on their hat, cloves, scarfs and coats, then ran outside to have a snowball fight.

Alfie and Bobby laughed and laughed as they tried hitting each other with snowballs, they then decided to build a snowman. They rolled the snow into two balls one larger then the other, they placed the smaller snow ball onto the larger one, just as uncle Thomas came out to join them, he had brought with him buttons for the eyes and mouth and a carrot for the nose, which the boys placed on the snowman while uncle Thomas placed a scarf around the neck and an old hat on its head.

The boys stood back to look at their snowman when whoosh a snowball came flying at them, that uncle Thomas had thrown hitting Bobby on the head, which started another snowball fight.
They played until they were too cold to play anymore and went back inside the lighthouse uncle Thomas made them all hot chocolate to warm them up, which they drank sitting by the fire. They stayed up late playing cards with uncle Thomas, because it was bobby's last night, as he was going home in the morning.

The boys thanked uncle Thomas for a wonderful day and said goodnight, then went to bed very tired.

Sadly for Alfie it was bobby's last night sleeping in the bedroom with him, "I'll be back soon", said Bobby, "I cant wait until the new year when I'll be back to go on more adventures with you, goodnight Alfie", "goodnight Bobby",Aflie replied, then they fell fast asleep.

CHAPTER 15

Christmas Eve

The boys were woken up early by uncle Thomas," Merry Christmas", he said as he walked into their bedroom, "but its not Christmas day until tomorrow uncle", said Alfie,"I know that laddie ", he replied, "but as Bobby is going home today I thought it would be nice to pretend it was Christmas day, come on you two I've made you a special breakfast and you can open your presents". "Hurray", shouted Bobby a he jumped out of bed, quickly putting his dressing gown and slippers on "come on Alfie hurry up", he said running down the stairs. Uncle Thomas laughed when Alfie jumped out of his bed to catch up with bobby. Uncle Thomas had made sausage and scrambled egg with toast for their breakfast, "yummy", said Bobby as he tucked in.

Alfie and Bobby started to clear away the breakfast things, as they had finished, "don't worry, leave that for now I'll do it when you boys get dressed", said uncle Thomas, "come and open your presents". The boys sat down on the floor as uncle passed them their presents, "open mine first boys", he said. They quickly unwrapped the present uncle Thomas had given to them, they each had a sword and a shield made out of wood, "thank you so much", they both said to uncle Thomas, showing each other their presents, uncle Thomas had carved their names on the shields and painted Alfie's red and Bobby's green. They wanted to go out and play with their new toys, until uncle Thomas reminded them that they were not dressed yet. It was the boy's turn next to give each other their presents they had made with a little help from uncle Thomas. Alfie let Bobby unwrap his present first, "Wow, that's really great", Bobby said to Alfie, "thanks", as he pretended to fly around the room, Alfie had made a toy aeroplane for him out of wood. It was Alfie's turn to open his present Bobby had given to him, it was wrapped up with an old comic, which made Alfie laugh, while he was unwrapping it. It was a toy car again made from wood, Bobby had painted it red, "its wonderful, thank you", Alfie said to his friend, "now its your turn uncle Thomas", said Alfie, "this is from both of us", he explained as he handed the present to his uncle, "ah boys you didn't have to get me anything", he said, "what a lovely surprise", uncle Thomas unwrapped his present to find a brand new penknife, "that's grand boys, I needed a new one thank you both very much, up you go now and get dressed", he said, "while I wash the dishes, if your quick you may have time to go outside and play with your new toys".

The boys rushed back up the stairs and got dressed very quickly, they put on their coats and went outside to play.

"Take that red knight", said Bobby to Alfie as he banged his wooden sword against Alfie's wooden shield, "oh no you don't green knight", said Alfie as he struck Bobby's shield with his sword. They played happily at being knights, fighting each other until uncle Thomas said it was time for Bobby to go, "fetch your toy aeroplane from the kitchen table Bobby while I carry your case down to the boat, you can say goodbye to Alfie" "I've got to go now Alfie", he said sadly, "thanks for my present, have a great Christmas, I'll see you in the new year". They ran down to the boat where uncle Thomas was waiting for them, "I have made a sandwich for your lunch Alfie", he said "cheer up laddie I'll be back soon with your mother who has another surprise for you". Alfie waved goodbye, then went back inside the lighthouse to play with his new toys.

Uncle Thomas took bobby to the train station where his mother was waiting for him, they were to catch the train to his auntie's home. "Bobby my baby", she said hugging and kissing him again and again, "ah mother", said Bobby wiping his face, but he really didn't mind he had missed his mother too. "Thank you for looking after him", his mother said to uncle Thomas, they said goodbye and boarded the train, "see you in the new year", Bobby shouted out of the train window to uncle Thomas as it was leaving the station. Uncle Thomas smiled and waved goodbye. Uncle Thomas returned to the shops to buy supplies for Christmas and not forgetting the turkey, while he waited for Alfie's mother and the surprise.

Back at the lighthouse Alfie got bored playing on his own he was used to having Bobby to play with. He ate his sandwich his uncle had left for him, them went for a walk a long the beach taking his penny whistle with him, it had been a while since he had seen dog so he blew into his whistle. Alfie heard dog barking from the cave, "I'm coming dog", he shouted running into the cave, once inside he found himself on a ship, not an ordinary ship but a pirate's ship, Alfie knew this because on the ship's flag was a black scull and crossbones, suddenly the cabin door swung open, "you there cabin boy", said the pirate with a patch over his eye, "come with me now". The pirate climbed down a rope ladder onto a small boat, Alfie did as he was told and followed the pirate onto the boat, "row", the pirate ordered, Alfie picked up the oars and started to row the boat across to the island.

When they reached the island the pirate jumped out of the boat and Alfie followed. "Me names one eyed jack", the pirate said to Alfie, "I've come for me treasure buried here and you will help me find it". "Yes sir", said Alfie "I have here a map, you take it and lead the way", said the pirate as he handed the map to Alfie, "Hurry cabin boy", he bellowed.

Alfie opened the map and saw markings drawn clearly to where the treasure was buried, as he looked closer at the map he recognized the tree they were standing in front off, he stood at the trunk of the tree where it showed on the map and said to the pirate "we need to tread twenty paces", he started to count as he walked, one, two, three until he reached twenty and stopped, "where next boy" said the pirate. Alfie looked around him then looked at the map, he saw a large pile of rocks on the ground which was identical to the picture on the map, "here" he said as he stood by the rock pile, "forty paces to the right", so he began to count again one, two, three four until he reached forty. They came to a beautiful waterfall, which was also drawn on the map with an arrow pointing to a cave behind the waterfall. Alfie began to walk through the waterfall to reach the cave, "wait boy", bellowed the pirate, he took out his sword and went a head in front of Alfie, "it's clear", he shouted, "you are safe to continue". Alfie followed him through the waterfall into the cave, which brought them out onto a bridge. "We have to cross over the bridge to the other side", said Alfie. The pirate went first and Alfie followed, "where to now", the pirate asked Alfie. Alfie checked the map again, there was a picture of a hill, he looked up at the pirate and said, "we have to go up to the top of the hill". Grumbling loudly the pirate began to climb the hill with Alfie behind him. They finally reached the top of the hill where large white stones were on the ground marked as a cross, "X marks the spot" said Alfie, "that is where your treasure is buried". The pirate began to dig with his bare hands moving the stones that were in the middle of the X, until finally he came across a small chest, he lifted it out of the hole and placed it on the ground beside him. He slowly opened up the treasure chest. Alfie gasped in amazement when he saw the chest was full of gold coins. The pirate threw one of the gold coins to Alfie and said "yours to keep for helping me found me treasure, now lets get back to me ship". Alfie quickly put the gold coin inside his pocket, then followed the pirate back down the hill, which was quicker then going up, over the bridge through the cave, under the waterfall and back to where they had left the boat. The pirate placed his treasure chest in the boat then climbed in, "jump aboard boy", he said to Alfie "I'll row us back to me ship". When they arrived back on board the ship dog was waiting there. Alfie waited for the pirate to go back inside his cabin with his treasure chest, he then blew into his whistle and they were home again, "happy Christmas ", he said to dog, before he was gone.

Alfie walked along the beach, putting his hands inside his pockets to keep warm he felt the gold coin the pirate had given to him, he quickly raced back inside the lighthouse and placed the gold coin inside his secret box his father had made for him.

Uncle Thomas had returned from the mainland, "we're home laddie", he shouted up the stairs, "I'm coming", replied Alfie, as he came down the stairs to welcome home his mother, he could not believe his eyes standing there on crutches beside his mother was his father, Alfie ran into his arms, hugging him tightly his father said, "its wonderful to see you son, you have grown so much since the last time I saw you". Alfie saw that his father was hurt and said, "what happened to you father"? His father explained to Alfie how he was hurt fighting in the war and was sent to the hospital on the mainland and how mother had nursed him better, "is that why you have not been able to come and see me mother", Alfie asked, "yes dear", his mother replied, " but we are all here now and it is going to be the best Christmas ever".

After supper they chatted and played cards, Alfie told his father how he found the penny whistle and all the magical adventures he has had, "you have to keep it a secret", he said, "you cannot tell anyone not even uncle Thomas or mother". Alfie's father promised.

Alfie's father went to bed early leaving Alfie and his mother making Christmas crackers for them all, she had brought with her four toilet roll holders and coloured paper, they placed some sweets inside the rolls, then wrapped a small piece of paper around the roll squeezing both ends to make them look like real Christmas crackers, "that is clever mother", he said. It was soon time for bed, Alfie placed the empty old sock of his fathers, his mother had given to him on his bedpost, ready for Santa, a picture of a snowman had been sewn onto it, he then got into bed and fell fast asleep.

CHAPTER 16

Christmas Day

Alfie woke up to a wonderful smell, it was Christmas day, he looked inside his Christmas sock and found presents from Santa, he found sweets and a chocolate bar, an orange, a book to read, a toy yoyo and a wooden truck. Alfie thought his presents were wonderful and raced downstairs to show his family.

"Merry Christmas Alfie" said his mother who was in the kitchen making breakfast, Alfie smelt the turkey cooking in the open, "mmmmm that's smells lovely mother", he said, "look what Santa brought me", he placed his presents on the table to show them. "They are lovely presents dear", his mother said, breakfast is ready, will you go and get uncle Thomas and father please". Alfie put his presents away and shouted" breakfast is ready". "Thanks laddie", said uncle Thomas, " Merry Christmas, yes merry Christmas son", said his father.

The family sat down at the table for breakfast, and afterwards opened their presents. Alfie's mother passed a present to uncle Thomas first, "this is from us" she said kissing him on the cheek. Uncle Thomas unwrapped his present to find two pairs of warm thick socks, Alfie's mother had knitted especially for him and a lovely warm jumper with a picture of a Reindeer on it, "their grand, thank you all very much", he said. It was fathers turn next, "this is from me", she said passing the present to him, he unwrapped it to find a scarf, gloves and a new wallet with a photo of her and Alfie inside it, "they are wonderful gifts thank you", he said.

"My turn", said Alfie, which made them all laugh, Alfie's mother passed to him two presents from them both, "here you son", she said, Alfie quickly unwrapped his presents and found a new puzzle and a board game to play later, and a wooden train set, just like the one he had played with when they went to Buckingham Palace and met daisy. "They are wonderful presents, just what I wanted, thank you very much", he then kissed his mother and father. Alfie's mother stood up to tidy away the breakfast things, "wait I have a present for you both", said Alfie, surprising his mother who had sat back down, he handed the small boxes to them, "one each", he proudly said, the blue box for his father and the pink box for his mother. They opened the boxes to find a small teddy bear each, with a blue scarf and a pink scarf around the necks, "they are so beautiful", said his mother, "thank you dear very much, what a lovely gift", said his father, "I will keep it with me always, thank you son".

Alfie helped his mother tidy up, them went and got dressed, "lets go outside and play in the snow laddie", said uncle Thomas, "while your mother prepares the Christmas dinner and your father can rest".
Alfie and uncle Thomas played outside in the snow until his mother called dinner is nearly ready. They came back inside, Alfie asked his mother if she would like help setting the table", that would be lovely dear", she replied.

They first placed the tablecloth onto the table, then his mother put a lighted candle in the middle of the table, Alfie helped to place the knives and forks and last of all the Christmas crackers they made together. " The table looks wonderful ", said his father, as they sat down to eat.

They had a lovely dinner turkey, roast potatoes, carrot and brussel sprouts, with lots of gravy. Everyone pulled their crackers and shouted BANG as they pretended to make the noise of real crackers, which made them laugh. After dinner uncle Thomas brought out the Christmas pudding, he had poured a little bit of brandy on top and lit it with his matches, "hurray", everyone said, as he placed the pudding on the table, that was Alfie's favourite, Christmas pudding and lots of custard.

Uncle Thomas washed up all the dishes for Alfie's mother because she had made such a wonderful dinner for them, then they all sat down and played Alfie's new board game and cards until it was time for bed.

The End

Printed in the United States
By Bookmasters